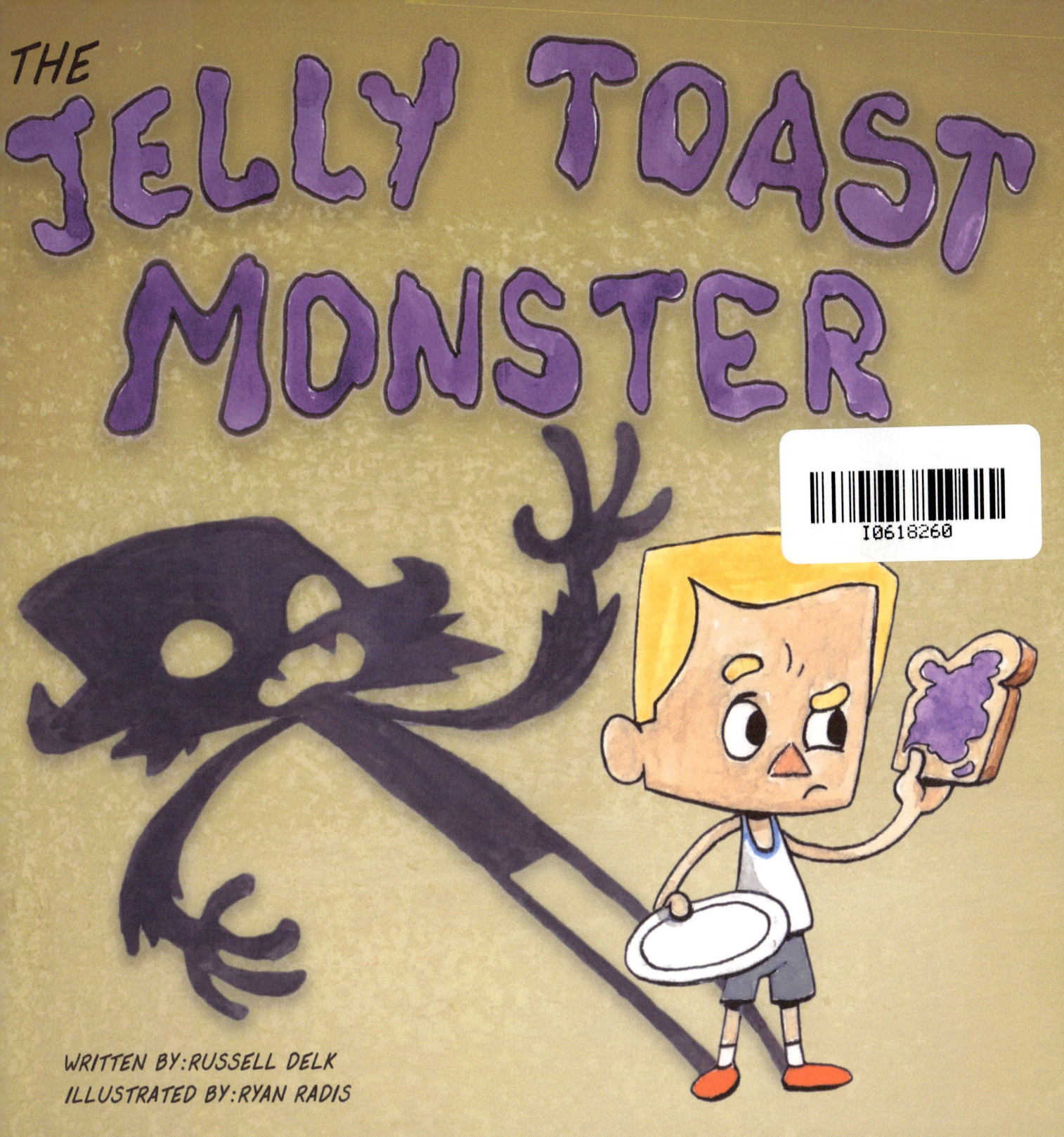

THE JELLY TOAST MONSTER

I0618260

WRITTEN BY: RUSSELL DELK
ILLUSTRATED BY: RYAN RADIS

For my son, Conrad.
I love you.

Published by Bobblehead Books, LLC Laurel, MS 39440

Text Copyright 2018 by Russell Delk
All Illustrations Copyright 2018 by Ryan Radis
All rights reserved.

Visit us on the web at www.bobbleheadbooks.com

All rights reserved. No part of this book may be reproduced or transmitted in any form or by any means, electronic or mechanical, including photocopying, recording, or by any information storage and retrieval system, without the written permission of the Publisher.

ISBN: 973-0998747637
ISBN: 0998747637

Printed in the United States of

America

The following story

is based on true events . . .

Breakfast time with Conrad was usually quick and easy.

Sometimes his Dad would fix him eggs or oatmeal.

But one day he made Conrad toast with just the right amount of JELLY.

Conrad loved the Toast but
more than anything,

the JELLY.

One day Conrad's dad brought him breakfast, but something was wrong.

As Conrad got more frustrated he began to change.

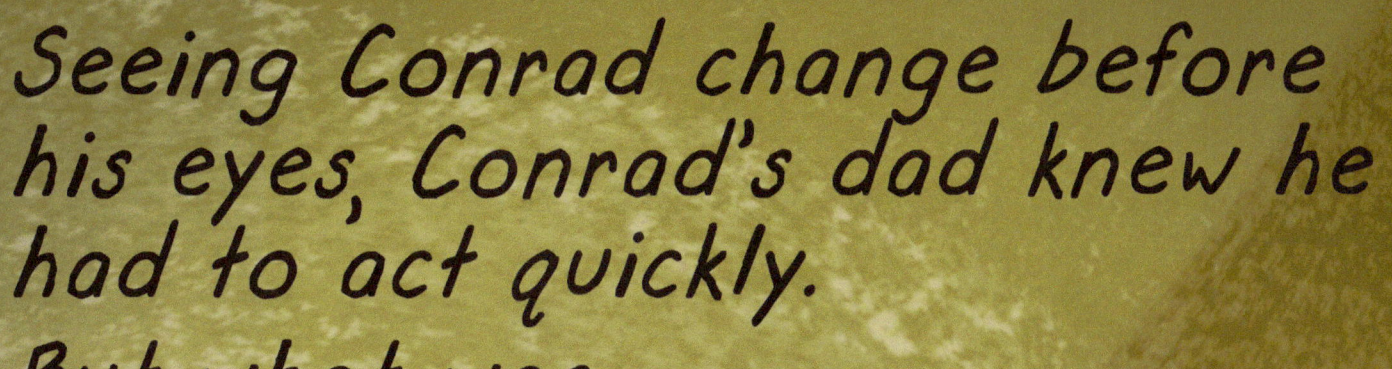

Seeing Conrad change before his eyes, Conrad's dad knew he had to act quickly.
But what was wrong with the toast?!

Conrad's dad looked at his son, but he didn't see Conrad. He was staring face to face with,

the JELLY TOAST MONSTER.

He had to bring his son back, but how?

He turned the toast over, "That should do it!"

The JELLY TOAST MONSTER threw his head back and howled with disapproval.

Conrad's dad yelled, "I have to try something else!"

He flipped the toast back over and put it on a different plate.

"That should do it!"

It did not.

The JELLY TOAST MONSTER jumped up and grabbed the light fixture, swinging and yelling.

"I have to try something else!"

He cut the toast into four
pieces and presented it to the
JELLY TOAST MONSTER.

"That should do it!"

It did not.

The JELLY TOAST MONSTER

inspected the toast and screamed.

"I have to try something else!"

He folded the jelly toast in half.

"That should do it!"

It did not. The JELLY TOAST MONSTER rejected that right away.

"I have to get this right!"

He added a piece of bread to make a sandwich.

"That should do it!"

Yet again, it did not.

The **JELLY TOAST MONSTER** climbed into the china cabinet and began smashing plates and cups!

Desperate, Conrad's dad cut the toast into eight bite sized pieces.

"This has to be it!"

The JELLY TOAST MONSTER took one look at the toast and immediately threw himself on the floor.

"I give up."
Conrad's dad picked up the toast and headed to the kitchen.

Seeing him leave, the JELLY TOAST MONSTER began to howl.

With one last attempt, Conrad's dad threw a piece of toast onto his plate. Lightly toasted with just the right amount of jelly. Jumping into his chair, the JELLY TOAST MONSTER examined the toast.

The fur began to disappear, the teeth began to shrink. And just like that. . .

CONRAD WAS BACK!

"Conrad, is it good?" His dad asked. Conrad smiled and nodded. The monster was gone, and the little boy enjoyed his jelly toast.

All the while looking forward . . .

To Lunch. . .

www.ingramcontent.com/pod-product-compliance
Lightning Source LLC
Chambersburg PA
CBHW041005170626
46815CB00002B/169